5217

HOLY FAMILY SCHOOL
232 Winchester Ave. Ashland, Ky.

T 6641

BIMBO
A Little Kinkajou

Written and Illustrated by
Theresa Kalab Smith

Steck-Vaughn Company • Austin, Texas
An Intext Publisher

ISBN 0-8114-7714-2
Library of Congress Catalog Card Number 74-110694
Copyright © 1970 by Steck-Vaughn Company, Austin, Texas
Printed and bound in the United States of America

"Do I see a monkey?
Or is it a bear?"

"Hello! I am Bimbo.
I am looking for the woods."

"Come with me.
I am going there.
I am Snoopy the raccoon.
Bimbo, are you a monkey?
Or are you a bear?"

"I am not a monkey.
I am called a honey bear.
But I am not a bear.
I am a kinkajou."

"A kinkajou!
I never knew a kinkajou.
Where is your home?"

"I came from Mexico.
I was a pet.
But I ran away."

"Bimbo, you walk like I do.
You walk like a little bear."

"At home in Mexico
I liked to swing in trees."

"In the day I liked to sleep.
At night I liked to play."

"Snoopy, look!
Trees! Trees!
Here I go up a tree!"

"Here I go after you!" said Snoopy.

12

"Bimbo, you can swing
from tree to tree.
I can go up a tree.
I can go down a tree.
But I cannot swing,"
Snoopy said.

"Shhhh! Look, Bimbo, there is a
mother deer and her baby.
The mother deer hears something.
See them run!"

"I'm hungry," said Bimbo.

"Let us go down, Bimbo, and find something to eat," said Snoopy.
"Down there is an old tree."

"Stop, Snoopy. Are these good to eat?"

"Yes, Bimbo, they are good to eat."

"I like to eat little bugs," said Snoopy.
"This old tree is full of little bugs."

"Come here, Bimbo.
I hear something!"

"What is it?" asked Bimbo.

"It is a bear! We must hide.
One never knows what a bear will do,"
said Snoopy.

"We can come out now.
The bear has gone, Bimbo.
Let us find some honey."

"HONEY! Do I like honey!"
said Bimbo.

"There is no honey here, Bimbo."

"There is some honey over here, Snoopy.
But the bees do not like us.
We take their honey,"
said Bimbo.

"There is a mother skunk!
See all her little skunks.
She shows them how to find bugs to eat,"
said Snoopy.

"I want to find more honey.
Come on, Bimbo. We must go!"

"Stop, Snoopy!
I see something!
What is it?"

"SNOW! It is snow!" said Snoopy.
"The first snow of winter!
See the animals run to their homes."

Bimbo and Snoopy see bears
and deer and skunks run by.

Even a mother opossum with four babies
runs to get away from the snow.

"Come, Bimbo, we must run with the
other animals. My face is cold,"
said Snoopy.

"I do not like the snow!"
cried Bimbo.
"I am going back to Mexico.
Good-by, Snoopy."

"Good-by, Bimbo.
I will remember you."

Bimbo is happy to be home again.
He likes to tell the story of his friend
Snoopy, and of the day he saw snow fall.